Why Should I
Switch Off the Light?

one small step

M J Knight

A⁺
Smart Apple Media

Smart Apple Media is published by Black Rabbit Books
P.O. Box 3263, Mankato, Minnesota 56002

Printed in China

Library of Congress Cataloging-in-Publication Data

Knight, M. J. (Mary-Jane)
     Why should I switch off the light? / M.J. Knight.
     p. cm. — (Smart Apple Media. One small step)
     Summary: "Facts about why saving energy is important and practical
tips for kids about how they can contribute to energy conservation"—
Provided by publisher.
     Includes bibliographical references and index.
     ISBN 978-1-59920-263-1 (hardcover)
     1. Energy conservation—Juvenile literature. 2. Power resources—
Juvenile literature. 3. Electric power—Conservation—Juvenile literature.
I. Title.
TJ163.35.K59 2009
333.791'6—dc22

                                                    2008011375

Designed by Guy Callaby
Edited by Jinny Johnson
Illustrations by Hel James
Picture research by Su Alexander

Picture acknowledgements
Title page Walter Geiersperger/Corbis; 5 Sebastien Desarmaux/
Godong/Corbis; 6 Robert Garvey/Corbis; 8 Liu Liqun/Corbis;
10 Gideon Mendel/Corbis; 11 Ashley Cooper/Corbis; 12 Dave.Houser/
Corbis; 13 Walter Geiersperger/Corbis; 14 Pablo Corral Vega/Corbis;
15 Steve Strike/epa/Corbis; 16 Corbis; 17 Colin McPherson/Corbis;
18 Bob Krist/Corbis; 20 Fridmar Damm/Zefa/Corbis; 21 Bob Krist;
22 Lester Lefkowitz/Corbis; 23 epa/Corbis; 24 Tim Wright/Corbis;
25 Clynt Garnham/Alamy; 26 DLILLC/Corbis; 27 Detail Parenting/
Alamy; 28 Rob Lewine/Corbis; Front cover: Chris Lomas/Getty Images

9 8 7 6 5 4 3 2 1

Contents

What Is Energy?

Energy is the power we use to give us light and warmth and to work machines.

We use energy from the world around us to make electricity and fuel so we can heat our homes, cook food, and travel. Burning plants, coal, oil, and gas are some of the ways we make energy.

Most of us can get the electricity we need just by pressing a switch.

One Small Fact

Every day up to 70 million barrels of oil are pumped out of the ground. We may run out of oil in about 40 years.

All over the world, people use energy to operate machines such as computers, as in this Internet café in Vietnam.

It costs a lot to capture energy, and it is easy to waste the energy we have. Every minute, all around the world, people are using huge amounts of electricity and fuel. Energy is being used up, and we have to find new ways to make the energy we need.

A Step in the Right Direction

You might think that what you do does not matter, but it does. It matters very much. Every time you think about how much energy you use or switch off a light when you leave a room, you take a step in the right direction. You can make a difference—everyone can. If lots of people take a step in the right direction, even a small one, these small steps will add up to one big step.

Where Does Our Energy Come From?

Our biggest source of energy is the sun. The energy in the sun travels to Earth as sunlight.

Energy from the sun is stored in plants and in fuels such as coal, oil, and natural gas. These are called fossil fuels and take millions of years to form. We burn these fuels in power stations to make electricity.

One Small Fact

More than 20 percent of the world's gas and oil come from under the ocean.

This rig in the sea off the south coast of Australia is drilling for natural gas in the ocean bed.

Where Does Coal Come From?

Millions of years ago, the sun shone on plants and trees growing in swamps. The plants took in the sun's energy. When they died, they fell into the swamps and lay there for millions of years. They were heated and compressed and gradually became the coal we burn for energy today.

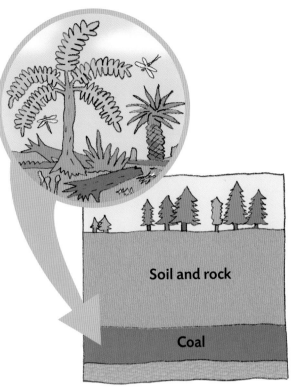

Soil and rock

Coal

Where Do Oil and Gas Come From?

Long ago, plants grew in the ocean using the sun's energy. Ocean creatures ate the plants. When the creatures died, their bodies drifted to the bottom of the ocean. They were covered in sand and mud and slowly compressed and heated over millions of years. Eventually, they became the gas and oil we use as fuel today.

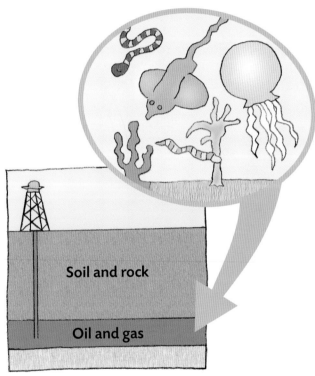

Soil and rock

Oil and gas

How Much Does it Cost?

How much would all the electricity used on Earth for just one minute cost? The answer is probably over 2 million dollars! We use electricity for so many things that people spend a fortune on it around the world.

Burning Fuel for Energy

There are some problems with getting our energy from fossil fuels.

One day, the supply of coal, oil, and gas will run out, so we need to look for other ways to get energy. Also, when we burn coal, oil, or gas, they give off gases. The gases mix with the air around us. This is part of a thick layer of gases around Earth called the atmosphere.

This power station in China burns coal, which gives off harmful gases into the atmosphere.

8

To stop Earth from getting hotter, we need to find ways of putting less gas into the atmosphere. One way we can do this is to use less energy in our daily lives.

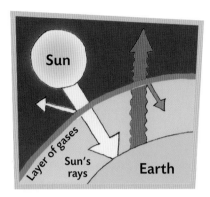

The atmosphere lets through the sun's rays, which keep Earth warm—but not too hot. The rays bounce off Earth and back into space.

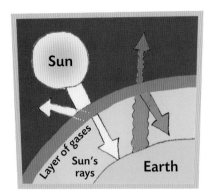

When the gases from burning fuel mix with the atmosphere, they keep more of the sun's heat near Earth. This means Earth is very slowly getting warmer.

I Can Make a Difference

Does your TV have a red light that glows even when it is switched off? That means it is on standby, ready to power up again quickly, and it is still using electricity. Many electrical items, such as DVD players and computers are like this. They can use half as much electricity on standby as when they are switched on. That is a lot of wasted energy. Help everyone remember to unplug or turn off your power strip. You will save energy and help save money on fuel bills too.

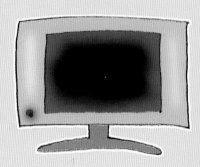

What's Happening to the Weather?

Have you noticed how the world's weather seems to be changing?

Warmer temperatures are causing big storms in some areas. Other places do not have enough water. The weather on Earth seems to be changing faster than ever before. Scientists call this climate change or global warming, and it is one of the reasons we need to be careful about the energy we use.

Very heavy rain caused serious flooding in parts of the UK in the summer of 2007. Scientists believe that such storms may be partly due to global warming.

As Earth gets warmer, some of the water, which is frozen as ice at the North and South Poles, is starting to melt and run into the oceans. In time, the melting ice will make the ocean water level rise. This could cause problems for people who live on low islands or near coasts that are not very high above the ocean.

The low-lying islands of Tuvalu in the Pacific Ocean may disappear under the ocean as water levels rise.

I Can Make a Difference

Does your family keep the house really warm so you can go around in T-shirts? Ask if you can turn the heat down just two degrees. You won't notice much difference and you can always put on a sweater, but you will use about 10 percent less energy.

Energy Without Burning

We do not have to burn fossil fuels in power stations to get energy.

We can use the sun's energy by catching it with solar panels. These catch sunlight and turn it into electricity that we can use in our homes.

Solar panels make most electricity on a sunny day, but they can still make some electricity when the weather is cloudy. Some power stations have been built that make electricity only using sunshine. Australia is building a solar power station that will be the biggest in the world.

One Small Fact

Enough energy comes to Earth from the sun in sunlight in 1 minute to give us all the energy we need.

A row of solar energy dishes reflects the heat of the sun at the White Cliffs solar power station in southern Australia.

I Can Make a Difference

Energy-saving light bulbs use up to 75 percent less energy than ordinary light bulbs and they last much longer. Ask your parents to change all the light bulbs in your home to energy-saving bulbs to save lots of energy. You can save even more by remembering to switch off the lights when you leave a room.

One of the best things about solar power stations is that they do not add harmful gases to the atmosphere. The energy we get from the sun is called renewable energy—it will never run out because the sun will not stop shining for millions of years.

This house in Austria has solar panels on the roof that harness energy from the sun.

Using Sunshine in the Rain Forest

In some parts of the world, people have electricity just by pressing a switch. But that is not true in many other places.

Children in a village in the Amazon rain forest in South America use electricity from solar panels. Their school has a special solar-powered unit. This makes electricity so they can use their computers. When it is dark, the solar energy lights the school and their basketball court.

Rain forests grow in parts of the world where it is warm and very wet, so there is plenty of sunshine to make solar power.

One Small Fact

If we covered just 1 percent of the Sahara Desert with solar panels, we could generate enough electricity for the entire world.

I Can Make a Difference

Do you have a dishwasher and a washing machine? Help your family make sure both have full loads before they are started. The machines use just as much water and energy whether they are full or only a quarter full.

Solar Races

The World Solar Challenge is a race held every year in Australia. The challenge is to design a car that will drive all the way across the country using only sunlight as fuel. Today, many countries hold solar races for boats as well as cars.

The Nuna 3 solar car won the Australian Solar Challenge race in 2005

Moon Power

Do you know that Earth and the moon pull toward each other like magnets?

The moon tries to pull Earth toward it, but the pull only makes a difference to the seas and oceans. The pull from the moon is what makes the oceans rise and fall on the shore when the tide goes in and out.

This photograph was taken from a space shuttle. It shows a full moon above the cloudy atmosphere of Earth.

I Can Make a Difference

Do you have a cell phone or an MP3 player? When you need to recharge them, leave the charger on just until you see the battery is fully charged, then unplug the charger. If the charger is left plugged in it will still use electricity and waste energy. For this reason, it is best not to leave things charging overnight. It is also a good idea to switch off cell phones at night. That way you will not have to recharge them so often.

We can use the energy made by the tides in tidal power stations. Making electricity this way does not add any harmful gases to the atmosphere.

The largest tidal power station in the world is in northern France. It makes enough electricity for 250,000 homes. Although this sounds like a lot, tidal power makes just a small amount—less than 1 percent—of the world's electricity.

One Small Fact

We can also use the energy from waves to make electricity.

The tide is very low on this beach.

high tide mark

The Power of the Wind

Another way to get energy is from wind. Sailors have always used the wind's energy to sail boats, and farmers once used windmills to grind corn.

This outrigger canoe uses the wind to sail between the many small islands of Micronesia in the Pacific Ocean.

Today, machines called wind turbines are used to make electricity. A wind turbine has large blades that move in the wind. The blades turn a machine called a generator that makes electricity. Many wind turbines together are called a wind farm. Some wind farms are built on land and some at sea. Wind turbines do not add to the harmful gases in the atmosphere.

The tallest wind turbines are built at sea. They can be 328 feet (100 m) high—taller than the Statue of Liberty in New York.

I Can Make a Difference

Some electricity suppliers get their energy from renewable sources such as wind power. You could find out which ones sell electricity to your electric company and ask your parents to use that supplier.

There's Energy Underground!

Did you know that deep below the surface Earth is very hot? We can use this heat to give us energy too.

Energy from underground is called geothermal energy. It is easiest to reach in places where there are earthquakes or near where there is a volcano.

The warm water in this thermal spring steams as it flows from underground.

In Iceland, people use geothermal energy to heat their homes and provide hot water. There are also hot pools people can swim in outside, even in winter. The water is heated from underground.

Geothermal power does not add to the harmful gases in the atmosphere, and it will never run out. So it is called renewable energy, like solar power and wind power. But geothermal power can be hard to reach. The countries that use the most geothermal energy are the United States, New Zealand, Italy, Iceland, and Mexico.

I Can Make a Difference

What uses the most electricity in your home? It is the refrigerator. If you leave the door open while you pour yourself a drink or grab a snack, up to a third of the cold air escapes. Then the refrigerator has to use more energy to get cold again. So remember not to leave the door open, even for a moment.

The water in this thermally heated pool in Iceland is warm enough for people to swim in it all year round.

Running Water

Have you ever seen a waterfall? We can use the energy made by falling water.

This energy is called hydropower. A dam is built across a river, stopping the water flow and making a lake called a reservoir. As the water runs from the lake through the dam, it turns machines to create electricity. The electricity is sent through cables to homes, schools, and offices.

Canada is the country that makes the most water power, followed by the United States, Russia, and Brazil. Norway produces almost all its energy from water.

Like solar and wind power, hydropower is a renewable source of energy. It does not add to the harmful gases in the atmosphere and it will never run out.

The Hoover Dam in the United States has generated hydropower from the Colorado River for more than 70 years.

The Three Gorges Dam in China will hold back enough water to fill 9 million swimming pools.

Biggest Dam

The world's biggest dam will be the Three Gorges Dam in China when it is finished in 2009. The dam is the most expensive thing ever to be built anywhere in the world.

Building the dam will make big changes to the land. More than 1 million people have to move from their homes to make way for the reservoir of water behind the dam.

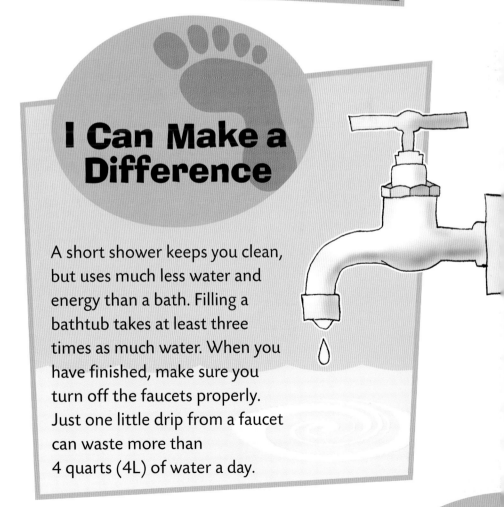

I Can Make a Difference

A short shower keeps you clean, but uses much less water and energy than a bath. Filling a bathtub takes at least three times as much water. When you have finished, make sure you turn off the faucets properly. Just one little drip from a faucet can waste more than 4 quarts (4L) of water a day.

More Energy

Some countries get a lot of their energy from nuclear power.

They use a metal called uranium that is dug up from the ground. Uranium is turned into nuclear fuel rods. At a nuclear power station, the rods are put into a tank of water where the uranium splits into smaller pieces and makes steam. This steam is used to make electricity.

This used nuclear fuel rod glows bright blue as it is cooled in a tank of water.

One Small Fact

France gets two-thirds of its energy from nuclear power.

I Can Make a Difference

Offer to help your parents hang the laundry so it can dry in the air. Tumble dryers use a lot of energy. If it is raining, you could help by hanging the laundry on a drying rack in the house.

Power from Waste

A power station in Norfolk, UK, makes enough electricity to heat 93,000 homes by burning 500,000 tons (450,000 t) of local chicken farm waste.

Burning Crops

Another way of getting energy is to burn biomass in power stations. Biomass is anything that was once alive. It can be trees or plants, animal waste, or food leftovers. But the trees and plants we burn are specially grown for this. New seedlings are quickly planted in their place.

Straw bales are unloaded at the world's biggest straw-burning power station in Cambridgeshire, UK.

How to Save Energy

As well as thinking about how we get energy, we can try to use less energy ourselves.

If we reuse and recycle things, we save the energy that is needed to make new things. Many of the things we use in our daily lives can be recycled: plastic bottles, cans, paper, cardboard, glass bottles, plastic bags – even toys, clothes, and computers. We can make 20 cans out of recycled material with the energy it takes to make 1 new can.

One Small Fact

Everyone throws away their own weight in trash every seven weeks.

The whole family can help when it comes to recycling the trash.

I Can Make a Difference

Check out how many bottles and cans your family use that can be recycled. Make sure you put them out for collection or visit the recycling center when you have a full bag or box.

When you want a new toy, why not buy one from a charity shop or neighborhood garage sale? This way you save the energy that goes into making a new one.

Recycling Energy Facts

The energy saved by recycling one glass bottle could power a light bulb for 4 hours.

The energy saved by recycling one plastic bottle could power a light bulb for 6 hours.

The energy saved by recycling one aluminum can could run a TV for 3 hours.

Saving Energy at School

Do you know how much energy your school uses?

Ask your teacher if you can do an energy survey to find out whether you can save energy at school. With some friends, visit every room to see where energy is being used.

Energy Project

Children at schools in India are taking part in a project to stop energy waste. Teams of children visit each classroom to check that no electricity is being wasted. Every classroom has a separate electricity fuse. If the team finds lights or fans switched on when no one is in the classroom, they take the fuse away for a day so the lights and fans won't work.

Check Out the Following

- **Lights:** Are they always switched off when no one is in the room?

- **Computers:** Are they shut down when they are not being used and overnight?

- **How are the classrooms heated? When is the heat switched on and off?**

- **Doors and windows:** Are any left open all the time? Does this waste energy?

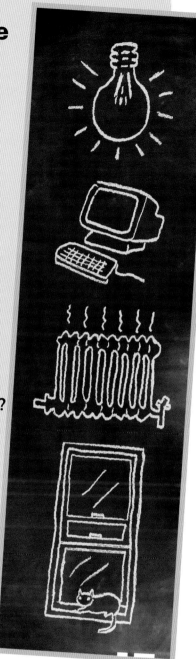

I Can Make a Difference

Why not set up an energy-saving club at school? You could meet at lunchtime and discuss ways to save energy like the children in India did or to use less energy in the first place.

Glossary

atmosphere
A thick layer of gases that surrounds Earth.

biomass
Anything that was once alive – plants, animal waste, or food leftovers.

fossil fuel
Coal, oil, and gas are all called fossil fuels. They were made over millions of years from living things. They are under the ground or the ocean.

geothermal
Geothermal energy is heat from inside Earth.

global warming
The gradual warming of the temperature of the air above Earth.

hydropower
Energy made by using the power of falling water.

nuclear power
Energy made using a metal called uranium in a nuclear power station.

power station
A building where electricity is made.

rain forest
A dense forest in parts of the world called the tropics, where the weather is very warm and wet.

renewable energy
Energy made from a source that will never run out. Solar power, wind power, and hydropower are all renewable sources of energy.

solar power
Energy made by using the power of sunshine.

tidal power
Energy made by using the power of moving water on coastlines as the tides come in and go out.

wind turbine
A giant windmill that catches the wind and uses it to make electricity.

Web Sites

http://www.depweb.state.pa.us/justforkids/
This Pennsylvania Department of Environmental Protection site has information on energy, water, and recycling.

http://www.eere.energy.gov/kids/
Learn about renewable kinds of energy on this U.S. Department of Energy Web site. Find out how to save energy and test your knowledge with games and quizzes.

http://www.eia.doe.gov/kids
The kid's page of the Energy Information Administration Web site provides energy information and games.

http://www.energyquest.ca.gov/saving_energy/index.html
This site offers kid-friendly energy saving tips.

http://epa.gov/climatechange/kids/index.html
Visit Recycle City provided by the U.S. Environmental Protection Agency. The site provides facts and games on recycling.

http://www.tvakids.com/whatistva/index.htm
This Tennessee Valley Authority (TVA) site has videos on wind and solar power. It also has activities on energy efficiency and global warming.

Index

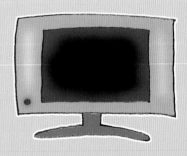